DEMAREST PUBLIC LIBRARY, NJ

3 9132 05016769 7

W9-BLQ-670

jF   grs.3-5
Ame
American Girls Collection
Kirsten saves the day

J'

Demarest Public Library
90 Hardenburgh Avenue
Demarest, New Jersey   07627

Demarest Public Library
Demarest, New Jersey

995-6/3/88

KIRSTEN SAVES THE DAY

A SUMMER STORY

BY JANET SHAW

ILLUSTRATIONS RENÉE GRAEF

VIGNETTES KEITH SKEEN

PLEASANT COMPANY

© Copyright 1988 by Pleasant Company
All rights reserved. No part of this book may be used or reproduced in
any manner whatsoever without written permission except in the case of
brief quotation embodied in critical articles and reviews. For information
address Pleasant Company, 7 North Pinckney Street,
Madison, Wisconsin 53703.
Printed in the United States of America
First Edition.

PICTURE CREDITS
The following individuals and organizations have generously given
permission to reprint illustrations contained in "Looking Back:"
pp. 62-63—Museum of the City of New York; Early Settler Life Series,
Crabtree Publishing Company, New York; Early Settler Life Series,
Crabtree Publishing Company, New York; pp. 64-65—Early Settler Life
Series, Crabtree Publishing Company, New York; Early Settler Life Series,
Crabtree Publishing Company, New York; Old World Wisconsin, State
Historical Society of Wisconsin; Early Settler Life Series, Crabtree
Publishing Company, New York; pp. 66-67—Early Settler Life Series,
Crabtree Publishing Company, New York; State Historical Society of
Wisconsin; Minnesota Historical Society; Mastai Collection, New York;
State Historical Society of Wisconsin.

Edited by Jeanne Thieme
Designed by Myland McRevey
Art Directed by Kathleen A. Brown

Library of Congress Cataloging-in-Publication Data

Shaw, Janet Beeler, 1937-
Kirsten saves the day: a summer story

by Janet Shaw; illustrations by Renée Graef; vignettes by Keith Skeen.
p. cm.—(The American girls collection)
Summary: Ten-year-old Kirsten is proud and excited when she finds a
bee tree full of honey, one of the natural treasures of her Minnesota
frontier world, but she exposes herself to great danger by trying to
harvest the honey by herself.
[1. Bee hunting—Fiction.   2. Frontier and pioneer life—Fiction.
3. Minnesota—Fiction.]
I. Graef, Renée, ill.   II. Title.   III. Series.
PZ7.S53423Kij 1988   [Fic]—dc19   88-2523
ISBN 0-937295-38-8
ISBN 0-937295-39-6 (pbk.)

FOR MY MOTHER,
NADINA FOWLER

TABLE OF CONTENTS

KIRSTEN

A ten-year-old who moves with her family to a new home on America's frontier in 1854.

PAPA, LARS, MAMA, PETER, AND BABY BRITTA

The Larsons sometimes long for Sweden, but they never lose heart for the challenges of pioneer life.

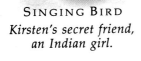

SINGING BIRD

*Kirsten's secret friend,
an Indian girl.*

MISS WINSTON

*Kirsten's teacher,
who lived with
Uncle Olav's family.*

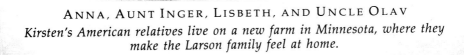

ANNA, AUNT INGER, LISBETH, AND UNCLE OLAV

*Kirsten's American relatives live on a new farm in Minnesota, where they
make the Larson family feel at home.*

THE BEE TREE

"We need enough fish for our supper, and for Uncle Olav's family, too," Mama told Kirsten and her little brother Peter. "That's fish for nine hungry people. Can you catch that many?" She handed them fishing poles and a willow basket to put the fish in when they caught them.

"Yes, Mama! We can catch all the fish you need," Kirsten said. "The stream is full of trout." The June day was warm and sunny, and she was eager to be on her way.

"Good! And take care of Peter," Mama added, looking straight at Kirsten. "The last time he went fishing with you, he chased a skunk."

Peter made a face. "I only did that once!" he said and picked up a small basket filled with the crickets they would use for bait.

With the baby on her shoulder, Mama walked with Kirsten and Peter to the path that crossed the meadow. "Remember, you've got bare feet, so watch for snakes," Mama said as they hurried ahead of her. "And keep a lookout for bears. Don't take any foolish chances."

"We'll be careful!" Kirsten called.

"Do you have your whistle?" Mama called back.

"Yes, Mama, I'll blow it if anything happens." Kirsten waved the wooden whistle her brother Lars had carved for her, then grinned at Peter. "Mama worries too much," she whispered.

Peter swung the bait basket. "Papa says that mothers are *supposed* to worry. Let's run, Kirsten!"

As they ran toward the stream the black-and-white puppy, Caro, dashed down the path after them. The pup leaped against Peter's legs and then Kirsten's skirt. "We should chase Caro back home," Kirsten said. "He might steal our fish, and Mama is counting on us to get enough for supper."

Peter knelt and scratched Caro's head. The pup swiped Peter's ear with his pink tongue. "Please let Caro come with us!" he said. "He likes the stream, just like we do."

Caro cocked his head and gazed up at Kirsten. He had a black spot over one eye and more spots on his back. "You're such a cute pup," Kirsten said. She turned to her brother. "But Peter, you know Caro will chase anything, even a snake. If he comes with us, you'll have to look after him. Can you take care of him and catch fish, too?"

"I'll take care of him!" Peter said. "I promise!"

So Caro tagged along. His white tail waved like a goose feather as he bounded through the grass, chasing blackbirds.

At the stream, Peter rolled up his pants. Kirsten tucked her skirt into the waistband of her apron and turned up the bottoms of her pantalettes. Caro splashed into the water to lap up a drink.

"Peter, call Caro!" Kirsten said. "He'll scare away the fish."

Peter whistled, and the pup jumped onto the bank and shook off a shower of drops. "See? He's a good puppy," Peter said. "He minds me, and I won't let him cause trouble." He handed Kirsten a cricket to bait her hook.

Kirsten waded slowly into the stream until the cool water came to her knees. The pebbles under her feet were soft with moss, and tiny fish tickled her ankles. She shivered with pleasure as she dropped her line into the water. She was glad the heavy work of spring cleaning and planting was over. Now, after school and on their free days, there was happier work to do. Like fishing! She thought there must be more trout here in Minnesota than anywhere in the world.

Peter baited his hook and followed Kirsten. Sweat ran from his yellow hair down his sunburned cheeks. "I wish we could swim instead of catch fish," he said. "Don't you wish we could go swimming, Kirsten?"

"I'd rather go fishing every single day!" Kirsten said. She squinted at Peter in the hot sun. Sweat ran down her forehead, too. "But I wish I had a straw hat like the ones Lisbeth and Anna wear. This sunbonnet is too warm." She loosened the sunbonnet ties under her chin, but still the damp cotton hat clung to her head.

Peter's willow pole dipped. "I've got a bite!" he cried. He pulled in a trout and held it for Kirsten to see.

The trout was dark green with orange and blue markings. Kirsten thought it was beautiful. "It's too small to keep, though," she said.

"But it's the only one we've caught, and we need lots and lots for dinner," Peter said.

"Papa says to throw the little ones back and let them grow," Kirsten reminded him. "We'll catch bigger fish in the deep pool upstream."

Peter tossed the fish back into the clear water, and they took their baskets and poles and waded upstream. Caro followed on the bank, sniffing at deer tracks.

Sure enough, the quiet pool was full of trout. It seemed that every time Kirsten or Peter dropped in a line, they caught one. Soon their basket was filled with fish.

Suddenly, the quiet was broken by Caro's shrill yelps of pain. "What's happened to Caro?" Kirsten cried. The pup dashed from the woods. He trembled all over, his tail between his legs. Still howling, he skidded to a stop on the bank and scuffed at his nose with both paws.

Kirsten and Peter splashed over to Caro. Peter dropped his pole and grabbed the frightened pup. "Kirsten, look at his nose!"

"He's been stung by a bee! Poor Caro! Hold him tightly, Peter!" Kirsten said.

Peter wrestled Caro still, then held the pup's head in both hands while Kirsten pulled out the stinger. "Poor puppy, poor puppy!" she whispered over and over against Caro's soft black ear. "I know it hurts, but I can make it better."

"I was going to take care of him, really I was!" Peter said. He looked as though he might cry. "But I was so busy catching fish, I didn't even notice when he wandered away."

"Don't worry, Caro will get over the sting," Kirsten said. She scratched the pup's chest as he licked and licked his nose. As she comforted him, she peered over his head at the deep woods where he'd wandered. The breeze smelled sweet, like blossoms. And in the distance, Kirsten thought she heard a faint hum, like the cat purring or Papa's

"He's been stung by a bee! Poor Caro!
Hold him tightly, Peter!" Kirsten said.

7

snore or maybe—bees. "I bet Caro found a bee
tree," she said softly.

"A *bee* tree?" Peter said. "What's a bee tree?"

"A bee tree is one with a hole in it, where bees
live. Listen!" Kirsten said.

Peter cocked his head the way Caro did when
he heard a whistle. "I do hear something
humming," he said after a moment.

"I think those are the bees!"
Kirsten said. "And do you smell
that sweet scent? It's basswood
blossoms. Papa told me that bees
love the blossoms on a basswood tree!"

"I smell blossoms," Peter said. "And I hear
bees. But why are you so happy about a tree full of
bees?" He rubbed his freckled cheek against Caro's
ear. "A bee *stung* Caro."

Kirsten jumped to her feet and brushed the
sand from her skirt. "Bees make *honey!*" she said.
"A bee tree will be packed full of honeycombs."

Peter took Caro in his arms and cradled him.
"What will we do with a tree full of honeycombs?"
he asked.

"We'll get them out of the tree and bring them

to Mama. She'll use the honey to make cakes and cookies!" Kirsten said.

"Cookies!" Peter grinned.

"A bee tree is good for more than just cookies, though." Kirsten tried to talk calmly, but as she thought about a bee tree she grew more and more excited. "Finding a bee tree is like finding a treasure. There's so much honey in a bee tree, Papa will be able to sell some of it at Mr. Berkhoff's store. Then Papa can buy the things we need this summer. I heard him say he doesn't have enough money for a saw and the cloth Mama needs and boots for Lars, too. If we bring Papa a whole tree full of honeycombs, he won't have to worry about money. I bet he'll be able to buy everything!"

Now Peter was on his feet, too. "Everything we need? Then let's get the honey, Kirsten!"

Kirsten pressed her finger to her lips and peered at the woods. "We can't just *get* honey. First we have to find the bee tree."

"It must be nearby. Caro got stung, and we both hear buzzing," Peter said softly, as though the bee tree was his idea to begin with. "Listen again."

She listened. Yes, humming came from deep in

the woods. "If we could find a bee tree, we'd make Mama and Papa so proud," she whispered.

"Let's go look for the bee tree!" Peter's blue eyes were wide with excitement.

Kirsten rolled down the hems of her pantalettes and untucked her skirt. "We can't both go look. One of us has to stay here with Caro so he won't follow along and get stung again. You said you'd take care of him."

Peter's mouth turned down as he petted the shivering pup. "If you find a bee tree, *you* might get stung, too. Mama told us to be careful."

"Oh, I'll be careful! I'm just going to look. Wait right here for me, and don't let anything else happen to Caro!"

Kirsten turned to the shadowy woods. She ran a little way, then she walked. Every few steps she paused, stood very still, and listened. At first the hum of the bees was fainter. She turned around and went the other way. Now the hum was louder and the scent of blossoms was stronger. She stopped again. Yes, buzzing and a sweet smell came from over there! She made her way slowly down the hillside through the thorny raspberry bramble.

At the bottom of the hill was a sunny clearing circled by a ring of trees. Across the clearing stood a basswood tree, its cream-colored blossoms loud with bees.

Kirsten crept closer. As she watched, a line of bees flew back and forth between the blossoms and a dead tree nearby. "The bee tree!" she said softly. She could hardly believe her luck.

The bee tree had a tall trunk with a jagged top. It was hollow, with a small opening just above Kirsten's head. Bees flew in and out of the opening. There were so many of them, thousands and thousands! They must be filling the whole tree with their honey!

"I've found a bee tree!" Kirsten whispered. "All by myself." It *was* like finding treasure. If she could bring this honey home, there would be plenty to cook with and lots more to sell at the store, too. Papa would buy the saw blade he needed, and Mama would get cloth to make new clothes, and Lars wouldn't have to go barefoot when he worked with the men. *Oh, I've got to get this honey*, Kirsten

11

said to herself. *There has to be a way, and I know I can find it.*

She carefully studied the bee tree. The opening was too high for her to reach unless she stood on a log. Maybe she'd have to climb a little, too. She saw that deep gashes scarred the trunk below the opening. Someone else had tried to climb the tree already. Someone else was after *her* honey!

Now Kirsten saw paw prints in the sand of the clearing. Bear paw prints! Bears were after her honey.

Kirsten backed slowly away from the bee tree and looked into the bushes. Papa and Mama had warned her many times to stay away from bears. But there was no sign of bears on this sunny morning. Probably the bears had gone away to another part of the woods and wouldn't come back. Anyway, this honey was hers, not the bears'. She had discovered it, and all she had to do now was figure out how to take it home.

She tried to think how Papa got honey from his beehives back in Sweden. She remembered he had used smoke to calm the bees, and he'd worn a veil to protect his head. Papa had packed his bee veil in

Someone else had tried to climb the tree already.
Someone else was after her honey!

the big trunk with the rest of the things they'd
brought to America. Probably the bee veil would
be in the barn. *If I use smoke and the bee veil, I
could get this honey all by myself,* Kirsten thought.

With a sharp stone she
scratched "K" on a birch tree
at the edge of the clearing.
Under her initial, she scratched,
"B tree." Now the tree belonged to her and no one
else could claim it. She ran
back to where Peter waited
for her.

"Peter, Peter, I was right!" she called as she ran
to the stream. "There *is* a bee tree!"

Peter sat cross-legged, the pup in his lap. A
frog hopped into the water as Kirsten scooted onto
the bank beside him. "Are you sure it's a bee tree?"
he said.

"Of course I'm sure! It's a hollow tree packed
full of bees! Oh, Peter, it's so big there must be
gallons of honey! Enough honey for cooking and
trading, too. We could get the honey, we could take
it home, we—"

"We could be stung just like Caro! Or worse!" Peter said. He frowned up at Kirsten. "If we fool with bees, we're asking for trouble. Let's tell Papa about the tree. He can get the honey."

"No, no! I can get it myself. I found the bee tree myself, didn't I?" She shoved her hands into her waist the way Mama did when she wanted strict attention. "Peter, are you afraid?"

Peter looked down at Caro. "I'm a little bit afraid," he said. "I bet you are, too."

"I am not afraid! I'm braver than you are," Kirsten boasted.

"Mama says that sometimes brave is another word for foolish," Peter said.

Kirsten grasped his shoulders. "Listen, I'm not a bit foolish! I *know* I can get that honey. If you don't want to help me, at least promise to keep the secret while I make a plan." She looked right into his blue eyes. "If you won't tell about the bee tree, I won't say you didn't take care of Caro."

Peter squinched up his mouth, but after a moment he nodded.

"Say *yes* out loud if you promise," Kirsten insisted.

15

"Yes," he whispered.

"Good! Oh, Peter, everyone is going to be so proud of me!"

IN THE
BERRY PATCH

"I love raspberry jelly!" Anna said. "I love raspberry jelly even more than I love maple syrup!"

"And your mama makes the very best jelly," Kirsten said. She and Peter were in the berry bramble near the woods, helping their cousins Anna and Lisbeth pick raspberries. Mama and Aunt Inger needed berries to make preserves today.

Peter's and Anna's mouths were red with raspberry juice because they ate almost as many berries as they put into their pails. Kirsten couldn't resist eating a small, plump berry now and then, either. She thought the berry juice was as sweet as honey. Everything made her think about honey and the bee tree these days.

"Our mama is going to sell her jelly and jam to Mr. Berkhoff," Lisbeth said. "And Anna and I are going to help her make berry pies to eat when we go to town for the Fourth of July." She smiled at Kirsten from under the shade of her straw hat. Little dots of sun filtered through the brim and scattered across her nose like freckles.

"What's the Fourth of July?" Kirsten asked. Her own cloth sunbonnet was heavy with sweat. Picking berries was hot work!

"The Fourth of July is the day the Declaration of Independence was signed. Do you remember when Miss Winston read the Declaration of Independence aloud in school?" Lisbeth put one hand over her heart the way Miss Winston did when she recited with feeling. "'Life, liberty, and the pursuit of happiness!'" she said. "I love that part!"

"Will we all go to town on the Fourth of July?" Kirsten asked.

Anna set her bucket down and wiped her chin with her apron. "Oh, yes! Everyone goes to town on the Fourth of July. The whole day is simply

18

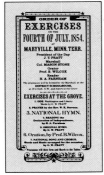

grand! There's a big parade with trumpets and drums. After the parade, there are speeches and music and a picnic, and contests and games, too."

Peter's face lit up. "Games? What kind of games?"

"Last year there was a three-legged race and a hurdle race," Anna said. "And a race to climb a greased pole. The prize was a whole dollar!" She pushed her straw hat back from her face. "The boys like the horse races, but I like the fireworks the very best."

"All day long guns and cannons boom and boom," Lisbeth said. "I don't like that so well."

"I'd love to hear the cannons!" Peter said. "Wa-boom! Wa-boom!" He made a fierce face that showed his berry-stained teeth. "And maybe I could win a running race."

Lisbeth looked doubtful. "Big boys run in those races, Peter. They'll run faster than you."

"But you could practice to run faster, Peter!" Anna said. "There are five more days until the Fourth." She held up five red-stained fingers.

Kirsten hadn't been thinking about the games and races. "Did you say people sell things in town on the Fourth of July?" she asked Lisbeth.

"Yes," Lisbeth said. "Everybody brings something to trade or sell. Last year we took sausages and spring chickens and butter, and preserves, too. Mama got a whole bolt of cloth, and there was even money left over. That's how Anna and I got our straw hats."

Kirsten's mind was back on the bee tree and the honey. She thought the Fourth of July would be the perfect time to sell honey in town. Maybe while everyone was busy picking berries, she could slip away into the woods for another look at her bee tree. If she was going to have that honey in five days, she'd have to work quickly.

Just beyond the raspberry patch were the deep woods where the bee tree was hidden. Kirsten moved along the berry bushes until she found a small opening she thought she could crawl through. No one saw her. They were still chattering about the fun on the Fourth of July.

Kirsten set down her berry bucket, got onto her hands and knees, and began to crawl through the bushes. Thorns pricked at her sleeves. She ducked lower until her elbows were on the ground. Her skirt rustled the leaves as she crept along.

Suddenly, right beside her, there was a loud snuffle. Alarmed, she stopped crawling. The snuffle came again, louder. When she turned, she looked right into the face of a black bear cub.

For a moment Kirsten couldn't get her breath. This was the first bear she'd seen up close. Papa had pointed out where bears slept through the winter. She'd seen bear tracks. But this round, furry thing was a *real* bear.

The cub stared at her from small, black-button eyes as it munched raspberries. As Kirsten stared back, the cub batted at a branch with its fat paw. Bits of leaves were caught in its thick fur. Kirsten felt herself smiling. The baby bear looked almost like a big puppy. She decided she had nothing to be afraid of. She thought it was even a good thing that the bear cub was up here in the berries, not over in the woods trying to raid the honey in her bee tree!

Then something startled the cub. It padded

clumsily out of the berry patch and into the woods. A moment later, Kirsten saw Lisbeth thrashing through the bushes.

"Kirsten? Where are you? You wandered off."

"I'm right here," Kirsten called. She tried to think of something to say so Lisbeth would stay where she was and not get any closer to the bee tree. "I thought the berries would be thicker here, but they're not."

As Kirsten moved toward Lisbeth, her foot hit her berry bucket. It tipped, and the berries spilled. She sat back on her heels to collect the spilled berries. "I just saw a bear cub. I think your footsteps frightened it away."

Lisbeth's mouth dropped open. "You saw *what?*"

"A little black bear cub," Kirsten said.

"Where did you see it?" Lisbeth said.

"It was right here in the bushes." Kirsten gathered a double handful of the spilled berries.

"Leave the berries, Kirsten!" Lisbeth whispered. "If there's a cub, the mother bear is sure to be nearby. She might come after us!" Lisbeth picked up Kirsten's empty bucket. "Let's go!" she hissed.

"We have to get out of here!"

"Don't worry, Lisbeth. The cub was alone. It was cute," Kirsten said.

Lisbeth took Kirsten's wrist. "Cubs look cute, but bears are wild animals, Kirsten! Stay far, far away from them. They won't bother us if we don't bother them."

"But I wasn't bothering the cub. We just looked at each other," Kirsten said. "Anyway, it's gone now."

"But I'm sure it went back to its mother, and mother bears are dangerous when they're taking care of their cubs! The mother bear would chase us if she thought we'd harm her baby. If she caught us, she'd use her teeth and her claws. Come on, we'll look for berries somewhere else!"

Lisbeth was almost thirteen, the oldest of the children. Kirsten knew she couldn't ignore what Lisbeth told her. She got to her feet and followed her cousin to a different part of the woods. As they walked, Kirsten said to herself, *Nothing will keep me from getting my honey, not even bears!* Still, she was glad the only bear she'd seen near the bee tree was a little bear.

BEARS!

The next morning, Kirsten stayed in the barn after she and Aunt Inger had finished milking the cows. As soon as she was alone, Kirsten searched for Papa's bee veil. She knew she'd need to wear it over her head to protect herself from bee stings. She found the veil on a shelf with the maple syrup buckets. She thought a syrup bucket would be good for carrying honey, so she took one. She took Aunt Inger's dipper, too. The only other thing she knew she'd need was smoke to make the bees drowsy and slow. She remembered that Papa had lit a torch near his hive back in Sweden. She decided she could burn a piece of pinewood for a torch. She would ask Peter to hold it.

Kirsten hid her supplies behind the barn and went to find Peter. He was down at the stream getting water for Mama. "Peter, you've got to help me!" Kirsten called.

"Help you do what?" he said.

"Help me get the honey from the bee tree. I've got everything we need to do it today."

Peter waded out of the stream with the full bucket. "Did Papa say we could?"

"I didn't ask Papa. I want it to be a surprise. I want to surprise everyone. Think of what Mama will say when we bring home a whole bucket full of honey!"

"*I'm* thinking of what Papa will say if you get hurt," Peter said.

"I won't get hurt! I know just what to do. And if you help me, I'll give you some of the honey for your very own. I bet you could sell it at Mr. Berkhoff's store and get that little knife you saw there. Then you could whittle just like Lars does."

"I'd like that little knife," Peter said slowly. But still he looked worried.

"Take the water to Mama, then meet me behind the barn," Kirsten said. "Don't let anyone see you." She ran off before he had a chance to argue.

After what seemed a long time, Peter came to where Kirsten waited. She took his hand and squeezed it hard. "Good for you, Peter!" she said. "I knew you'd be brave enough to come with me! Here, take the dipper."

Right behind Peter came Caro. The pup jumped against Kirsten's legs. "Go home, Caro!" Kirsten whispered. "Shoo!" But Caro wouldn't go home. He licked Kirsten's hands and barked with excitement, as if he were in on the secret.

"He wants to come with us. Can't he help, too?" Peter asked.

"Well, I suppose he could stand guard for us. If bears come near the bee tree, Caro can chase them away," Kirsten said.

"*Bears?*" asked Peter.

"I just mean there are bears in the woods, and bears like honey, that's all," Kirsten said quickly. "There's nothing to be scared about. Let's go!"

Kirsten led the way into the forest. She and

Peter and the pup climbed a steep hill, then went down the other side. Soon they could hear the sound of the bee tree. "Listen to that hum, Peter! We're almost there," Kirsten said.

When Peter saw the bee tree and heard its loud hum, his eyes went wide. "I didn't know there were so many bees in the whole world!" he said. Caro dashed around the clearing. He sniffed the ground, but being stung had taught him not to go anywhere near the bees.

Kirsten set the bucket by her feet and picked up a pinewood stick for a torch. "You'll hold the torch right by the hive to keep the bees quiet while I dip out the honey," she told Peter. "But first I have to put on the bee veil."

"Can I get under the veil with you?" he asked in a small voice.

"You can stand under the veil if you keep one hand out to hold the torch. Roll down your shirt sleeves, Peter."

As Peter started to roll down his sleeves, Caro began to bark fiercely. Nearby, twigs cracked as something moved in the bushes. Caro ran toward the noise, yipping. Then the bear cub tumbled out of the thicket, with Caro right behind!

"Oh, no!" Kirsten cried. She
dropped the bee veil in alarm.
She hoped the cub was alone
again. She hoped its mother
wasn't near, because if a mother
bear saw Caro chasing her cub, there would
be trouble. The bear would think her cub was in
danger and come after them all. Kirsten shook her
apron and called to Caro. "Caro, stop it! Stop!
Leave the cub alone!"

Caro turned to face the cub and bared his
teeth. The cub growled back. Caro snapped and
the cub showed its sharp teeth. They were going
to fight!

"We've got to get Caro, Peter!" Kirsten cried.
"Quick, quick!"

"Come, Caro!" Peter yelled. He picked up a
stone and threw it at the cub. "And you, bear, you
scat!"

Just then a deep growl echoed through the
forest. Something huge broke from the shadows.
The mother bear rushed to protect her cub! She
lumbered swiftly forward, her head swinging. She

Just then a deep growl echoed through the forest.
Something huge broke from the shadows.

snorted at Caro, then flipped the pup away from her cub with a swift blow of her shaggy paw.

Caro yelped in pain as he landed in a pile of leaves. Then he was on his feet, streaking back home the way they'd come.

The bear turned to lick her cub, and Kirsten realized she and Peter had just this one chance to get away. She grabbed Peter's hand. "Quick! Climb that tree!"

They raced to the far side of the clearing. Kirsten made a step for Peter with her clasped hands. He jumped into it and stretched for the lowest branch of a big oak. He caught it, and Kirsten boosted him until he got a good grip. Peter dangled a moment, she shoved, and he threw his leg over and scrambled up onto the branch.

"Climb fast!" Kirsten cried. "Don't stop!"

"You come too!" Peter said. "Here's my hand!"

She grasped his hand and the branch and struggled up after him. Bits of bark showered into her face as they climbed higher up the tree.

The mother bear nuzzled her cub. Then she stepped in front of it and looked around the clearing again. Kirsten's ears hummed like the bees in the bee tree. Everyone knew black bears climbed trees easily. The bear could come right up this tree after them!

Again and again the mother bear shook her head, growling and snorting. Then she charged toward the tree, her paws slapping the ground like drumbeats. She stopped about ten feet away and peered up into the branches where Kirsten and Peter hung on.

"Dear God, please make the bear go away," Peter prayed. His eyes were tightly closed.

But Kirsten couldn't take her gaze from the bear. She could see the sharp teeth and long claws. It was so close she could smell the musky stink of its fur. If the bear came up the tree, she and Peter wouldn't have a chance.

Slowly, still watching the tree, the mother bear rose up on her hind legs. Her thick fur hung like a black robe as she sniffed the air. Then she lowered herself down onto all fours again and began to back up toward her cub.

When she reached the cub, the big bear gave it a swat as if to say, "Mind your mother!" The

cub scuffled into the woods and its mother
followed, looking back once over her heavy
shoulder. The branches closed behind them, and
they were gone.

Kirsten let her breath out very, very slowly.
"Peter?"

"Are we still alive?" he whispered.

"The bear went away," Kirsten said. "Open
your eyes."

Peter squinted two thin slits of blue. "Will it
come back?"

"I don't know," Kirsten said softly. She got a
better grip on the branch she held.

"I'm afraid to climb down," Peter said.

"Me too." Kirsten tried to swallow, but her
mouth was too dry.

"Oh, Kirsten, the bear hurt Caro!"

"Caro could still run. He'll be all right. Don't
cry," Kirsten said. But she felt tears on her own
cheeks. She bit her lips and looked down at the
claw marks in the dirt below them, then at the deep
scratches around the bee tree. What if the bear
came back? Oh, why had she decided to come here
with no one but Peter? Why did she think she

could get the honey herself? Why hadn't she been more careful?

Kirsten and Peter were still clutching the highest branch of the oak tree they'd climbed when they heard someone shouting in the distance, "Kirsten! Peter! Where are you?"

"It's Papa!" Peter cried.

"Here!" Kirsten called back to him. "We're here, Papa!" She remembered the whistle she wore around her neck and blew three short blasts.

Papa called again. His voice was closer now. Then he strode into the clearing, carrying his big rifle.

Peter began to skid and slide down the tree to him, but Kirsten stayed back. "Watch out, Papa!" she cried. "A bear chased us! It might be close by." She looked down through the leaves at Papa's red face.

Papa set his rifle against the tree. "I've got my gun. But no bear would come near this noise. They want to keep away from us as much as we do from them. You two come down here!"

Peter jumped from the lowest branch into Papa's arms, but Kirsten was almost as afraid of

Papa as she had been of the bear. Papa sounded very angry.

"Are you all right?" he asked Peter.

Peter nodded.

"Kirsten, are you all right?"

"Yes, Papa," she said.

"How did you find us?" Peter said. He held on to Papa's neck.

"The pup came home with his leg bleeding," Papa said. "It looked like a bear had clawed him. I know he likes to tag along with you, and I was afraid you'd met up with bears. So I grabbed my gun and followed the trail of his blood back through the woods. Then I heard your shouts and the whistle." He set Peter on the ground and held his arms up to Kirsten.

She jumped down, her face hot. Papa set her on the ground and took her shoulder in his strong grip. "Tell me what you're doing here," he said sternly. When Papa was angry, his eyes seemed to burn like the fire in the cookstove.

Kirsten kept her gaze on her dusty feet. "I found that bee tree, Papa," she said.

He glanced at it for the first time. "Well, that's a good find. Go on."

"It's full of honey," Kirsten said. "Peter and I wanted to get the honey for you. We thought you could sell it at the store." She tried to smile, but her lips felt numb.

"And you went to get it by yourselves?" Papa asked.

"Kirsten said she knew what to do, and that we could surprise you!" Peter said.

"You agreed, Peter. You said yes!" Kirsten hissed.

"Then Caro chased a cub, and the big bear

36

came," Peter hurried on.

Papa stroked his beard. There were deep furrows in his brow, like the ones his plow made in the field. "Did you know bears came to the bee tree, Kirsten?"

"I saw a bear once, but only a baby," she murmured.

"But you know mother bears are always near their cubs to protect them! You did a very, very foolish thing! You put your life and Peter's life in danger! You've got to be careful in the woods!" Papa's voice boomed.

Peter pushed between Papa and Kirsten. "But Kirsten saved my life! When the big bear came, she helped me up in the tree so I'd be safe! She was very brave!"

Papa took Peter's hand, then Kirsten's. "Listen to me! It isn't brave to go near bears, it's dangerous! The only way to be safe from bears is to stay away from them. And never, never go near the cubs, do you hear me?"

"I'm sorry, Papa." Kirsten could hardly hear her own voice.

"We thought you'd be happy about a bee tree," Peter whispered.

"We thought that if we brought you the honey, you'd be able to get all the things you need at Mr. Berkhoff's store," Kirsten added.

"The honey in this tree will be valuable, I'm sure of that," Papa said. "But the bees are an even better find." Papa looked stern. "If you had broken into the hive with that dipper, you would have destroyed the colony of bees. You might have ruined the honey, too. And what's much worse, you'd have been badly stung! Kirsten, you're ten years old! You're old enough to take good care of yourself and your little brother. You're old enough to know better!"

Kirsten was ashamed. Because of her recklessness she'd put Peter in danger. The pup had been clawed. Mama and Papa were frightened and upset. And she had almost destroyed the treasure she'd found. She couldn't keep tears from rolling down her cheeks. "Oh, Papa, I'm so sorry! Truly I am!"

Papa leaned down and looked into her eyes. "I can see I don't need to paddle you. You've been

punished enough. Come home now." He picked up
the bee veil and the syrup bucket, then his rifle.
"I'll come back tomorrow and take the honey *and*
the bees to the farm."

BRINGING BACK
THE BEES

"Do you have the saw?" Papa asked Lars.

"Yes, I have it," Lars said. He lifted the big saw onto his shoulder.

Kirsten and Peter watched from where they sat in the barn loft. Today Papa and Lars were going to saw down the bee tree and move the colony of bees back to the farm. A round straw skep would be the bees' new home. Papa and Lars would set it in the meadow near the barn, and the bees would fill the skep with honeycombs. By fall, Papa would be able to harvest more honey.

"Why are we taking the bellows?" Lars asked.

"Smoke will calm the bees before we move

them," Papa said. "We need the bellows to blow the smoke inside the bee tree."

"See, our torch wouldn't have worked anyway," Peter whispered to Kirsten.

She didn't answer him. She had her chin in her hands, and she was thinking. When she shut her eyes, she remembered the bear rushing at the tree where she and Peter hid. She didn't like to have these bad memories. "I should go back to the clearing where the bear chased us," she said very softly.

Peter sat on his heels and stared at her. "Why do you want to go back? It was terrible to be chased!" He put his hand on her forehead the way Mama did when they were sick. "Do you have a fever?"

"No, I don't have a fever. But I dreamed about bears last night," Kirsten said. "I think if I don't go back to the woods today, I won't ever have the nerve to go again."

"Well, I'm not going, not even with Papa and Lars," Peter said firmly.

When Papa picked up the bee veils, Kirsten climbed down the ladder. "I can carry those for you, Papa," she said. "You have to carry the skep."

Papa raised his eyebrows. "Are you asking to come with me and Lars?"

Kirsten nodded. She thought Papa was still angry at her, because she hadn't seen him smile since he had found her and Peter in the tree yesterday. "Could I come with you, please?"

Lars scratched his blond head. "Aren't you afraid of the bears, Kirsten?"

Lars was fifteen, and it seemed to Kirsten that he wasn't afraid of anything in the world. "Yes, I'm afraid," she said. She could barely hear her own voice. "But I think I'll be less afraid if I go back with you and Papa."

Lars grinned at her. But Papa said sternly, "Moving bees isn't play, Kirsten."

"I know, Papa," she said.

"If you come with us, will you do exactly as I tell you?" Papa asked.

"I will. I'll do exactly as you tell me." Kirsten grabbed the bee veils. She glanced up at Peter, who sat at the top of the ladder with his arms around his knees.

"Could Peter come, too?" she asked Papa.

Before Papa could answer,
Peter said, "I'm going to stay
home and look after Caro!"

Papa took the straw skep in his arms. "Peter,
tell your mother that Kirsten is going with me and
Lars. Mama's not to worry. Kirsten will be safe with
us."

Peter slid down the ladder and ran to the
house. Kirsten followed Papa and Lars back to the
woods.

At the clearing, Papa took Kirsten's hand and
led her to a spot across the open space from the bee
tree. He drew a mark on the ground with the toe of
his boot. "Stay right here, Kirsten. Don't come even
a single step closer to the bee tree," Papa said.

Kirsten stood right on the mark Papa had
drawn. Sunlight slanted through the trees, and the
air smelled of basswood blossoms. But even on this
pretty morning it was easy to remember the mother
bear snorting and pawing here. Kirsten watched
Papa and Lars closely, so that she wouldn't think
too much about the bear.

They put the veils over their hats and pulled
them down to cover their faces. Then Papa started

a fire by the bee tree. When the fire was going, Lars used the bellows to pump smoke inside the hole. Big puffs of black smoke disappeared into the hollow of the bee tree. At first the bees buzzed more loudly. Then they were quieter, as though they might have fallen asleep.

"Now," Papa said to Lars, "we'll saw off the top of the tree."

They each took an end of the saw and began to cut the dead tree just above the place where the bees lived. Soon the tree top crashed into the clearing. Kirsten looked over her shoulder. If any bears were near, that thud would scare them away.

Quickly, Papa put the straw skep over the part of the tree that was still standing. He thumped the tree to move the bees up into the skep. When he thought that all the bees were inside, he lifted the skep onto a long board. Then he and Lars took the saw again. They cut a thick log from the stump. It was filled with combs of honey. They loaded the log full of honey onto the board, too, and each picked up an end.

"Let's head for home," Papa said.

As they left the clearing, Kirsten looked around

*Quickly, Papa put the straw skep
over the part of the tree that was still standing.*

one last time. She wasn't so frightened now. She knew there were bears in the forest and that they would always be here. But she knew, too, that she could be wise and careful. If she didn't bother them, the bears would stay away. She ran to catch up with Papa and Lars.

When they got back to the farm, Papa and Lars put the bee skep on a platform in the meadow. Then they carried the log full of honey back to the cabin. Mama was waiting there with hot water to melt the waxy honeycombs. Peter was scrubbing out crocks to fill with honey.

Kirsten stood a little way away, watching.

"Is it a big colony of bees?" Mama asked Papa.

"It's a good, big one!" Papa said. "It will make lots more honey. And look at all the honey in this log now. Even if we keep enough for cooking, there will be plenty to sell in town on Tuesday."

Mama clasped her hands in pleasure. Kirsten could see that Mama was happy. Still, that didn't make Kirsten feel as proud about the honey as she'd expected to be.

As though she read Kirsten's mind, Mama

turned to her. "Why are you looking so sad, dear?" Mama said.

"I thought *I* could get the honey for you," Kirsten blurted out. "I thought I could do it myself. I wanted to help you get the things we need from Mr. Berkhoff's store. But instead of helping . . ." Suddenly she couldn't talk anymore. Her eyes blurred with tears. She had nothing to be proud of after all. It had taken Papa and Lars to get the honey. All she'd done was to put herself and Peter in danger. And Caro had been clawed. Tears dripped off her face onto her dress.

Mama's arm went around Kirsten's shoulders. "I'm proud of you for finding the bee tree. Papa and I know you wanted to help. And you *did* help. You found us good honey to use this summer, and enough to sell in town, too. And since your papa brought the bees home, we can count on having more honey next fall. All because of you, Kirsten." Mama gave her a squeeze. "Now we have work to do to get this honey ready to sell on the Fourth of July. We're going to need your help again."

Kirsten blinked at Mama through her tears. She wanted to be just like Mama when she grew up.

"You're a smart girl, Kirsten," Papa said. He wiped tears from her chin with his thumb. "And you're certainly brave. Nothing seems to scare you. You just have to remember to be brave *and* careful at the same time." Papa's smile told her everything was all right.

CHAPTER
FIVE

THE BEST
BASSWOOD HONEY

"Get your sunbonnet, Kirsten!" Anna
called. "The wagon's hitched! It's time
to go to town!"

Kirsten emptied the dishwater on the garden
behind the little cabin. She wiped her hands,
grabbed her sunbonnet, and hurried out to the
wagon. It was loaded with crates of chickens,
baskets filled with sausages, jars of jelly, and two
big crocks of Kirsten's honey. Papa, Lars, and Uncle
Olav were squeezed into the front seat. Mama and
Aunt Inger were on chairs behind them. Mama held
the baby in her arms.

Kirsten scrambled up onto the very back of the
wagon, beside Peter. They sat with their feet

dangling over the back board, crowded in beside the big picnic hampers. As the wagon rolled down the road, crows swooped overhead and dust billowed behind the wheels. From behind the wagon came a high-pitched yip yip yip.

"Caro's chasing the wagon!" Peter cried.

"Papa, please stop!" Kirsten called.

Papa reined in the horses. Caro appeared out of the dust, his pink tongue lolling. He jumped against the wagon wheel and wagged his tail.

"Even with his hurt leg he chased us!" Peter said. He climbed down and petted the pup.

"He must want to go with us very badly," Kirsten said. "Could we take him along, Papa?"

"There will be a lot of dogs in town today," Papa said. "Caro might get in a dog fight. He'll be better off on the farm, Kirsten."

"But I'll tie a piece of rope around his neck and keep him close to us," Kirsten begged.

"We'll take good care of him!" Peter chimed in.

"I suppose that two children should be able to manage one puppy," Papa said. "Bring him up in the wagon, Peter. Let's go."

Caro settled on Kirsten's lap. "We'll look after

you, I promise," she whispered against his silky ear.

Soon the Larsons' wagon was joined by many other wagons on the road to Maryville. Everyone shouted and laughed and waved to one another through the dust.

"Isn't the Fourth of July grand?" Anna cried. "It's almost like Christmas in the summer!"

"I can already hear the guns and cannons in town!" Peter said.

The streets of Maryville were crowded with wagons and buggies. People filled the lanes and the little park in the center of town. Papa found a place near Mr. Berkhoff's store to unhitch the horses. Everyone climbed off the wagon. Then Papa, Uncle Olav, and Lars began to unpack the boxes and crates.

Before they finished, Mr. Berkhoff came out of his store. He wiped his hands on his apron as he looked over the goods the Larsons had to sell him. "What have you got for me?" he said. "More of your good sausages, I see."

"And raspberry preserves and maple syrup, too!" Aunt Inger stepped forward to show off what they had brought. She was good at making a bargain.

Mr. Berkhoff bent down to peer into the crates of chickens. "More hens? I'm not sure I can take more hens. Everyone seems to have brought them to market today."

"Not as plump as these hens," Aunt Inger said quickly. She stood right by Mr. Berkhoff's side. "We raise the plumpest chickens! And take a look at the wheels of cheese. You don't see cheese like ours every day. It's surely worth a lot." She smiled confidently.

But Mr. Berkhoff scratched the bald spot on his head and frowned. "Well, that depends on what you folks will be wanting to buy."

"Cloth!" Mama and Aunt Inger spoke at the same time.

"But first we need boots for our Lars, and a saw blade and nails," Mama added.

Mr. Berkhoff glanced at Lars, who lifted baskets from the wagon. "That boy has grown a foot taller since I saw him last," he said. "I hope I've got boots big enough! Did you bring any more of your little wood carvings to sell, Lars? One of the town ladies asked about them."

Lars' cheeks turned red. He wasn't used to being praised. "I brought a few carvings," he said.

"Good!" Mr. Berkhoff said. But still he didn't smile as he looked over the stacks of boxes and crates. He seemed to be adding them up in his head.

Peter leaned against Kirsten's side. He whispered, "Shall I ask Mr. Berkhoff about the little knife, so I can learn to carve like Lars?"

Kirsten pinched Peter's arm. "Hush, Peter! We might not even have enough money for what we need. We won't be able to buy any extra things."

"But you *said*," he murmured. Then he pressed his lips together. He knew as well as Kirsten did that the important things like a saw blade and boots came first.

Now Aunt Inger pushed forward the crate that held the boxes of beeswax and crocks of honey. "I've saved a surprise for last, Mr. Berkhoff!" she said with the same excited voice she used when she served her special cake for Sunday dinner.

Kirsten pinched Peter's arm. "Hush, Peter!" she said.
"We might not even have enough money for what we need."

Mr. Berkhoff's gray eyebrows went up as she handed him a box of the beeswax. "What's this? Beeswax!" he said.

"It's fine, clean wax, as you can see," Aunt Inger said.

A little smile pushed up the corners of Mr. Berkhoff's lips. "This beeswax will sell for candles and for furniture polish, too. The town is growing, you know. Some fine ladies who have time to polish their furniture are moving here."

Papa held up one of the crocks of honey. He pulled off the cork and offered the crock to Mr. Berkhoff. "And here's honey, too. Basswood honey. Why don't you have a taste?"

Mr. Berkhoff dipped his finger into the crock, licked the honey, and a grin spread across his red face. "Where did you get such fine honey, Mr. Larson?"

"Our Kirsten has a nose as good as a bear's for honey!" Papa said. "She found a bee tree in the forest and we moved the hive to our farm." He pulled out his handkerchief and wiped his forehead. "What do you think of it?"

"Delicious!" said Mr. Berkhoff. He took another

 taste and then another. "So Kirsten found this honey! You can bet I'll tell folks who buy it where it came from. We don't often get such pure basswood honey." He smiled at Kirsten. "This will be worth something, young lady."

She wanted to smile back, but she was still too worried to feel happy. Even with the honey, maybe there wouldn't be enough to buy what they needed.

"You women go inside the store and look over my pretty new calico," Mr. Berkhoff said to Mama and Aunt Inger. "The men will finish up out here, and we'll settle our accounts."

Mama and Aunt Inger made their way through the crowd in front of the store. Anna and Lisbeth went right behind them. Kirsten and Peter tied Caro in the wagon where he'd be safe, then ran to catch up to the others.

As Kirsten stepped inside the door, she smelled the mouth-watering scents of spices and coffee and sausages. The little store hummed as loudly as a beehive with the voices of the shoppers. Mama and Aunt Inger joined the women who unrolled bolts of cloth on the wide counter. Anna bent over the candy display and Lisbeth looked at lace.

"I'm going to look at pocket knives," Peter said to Kirsten. "It won't hurt just to *look,* will it?"

She gave him a little shove toward the display of knives. "Pretend you can have any knife you choose," she said. "Pretending won't hurt."

Kirsten stopped by Lisbeth to run her finger along a length of pink ribbon. On the shelf above the spools of ribbons was a broad-brimmed straw sun hat like the one Lisbeth wore. Gently, Kirsten traced the wide brim of the new hat. *If I could have anything in the store, I'd pick this straw hat,* she thought. *It would be so cool and so pretty on these hot summer days.*

Papa's voice boomed from behind her. "Do you need two hats, Kirsten? Isn't your sunbonnet warm enough for you?"

Kirsten could tell he was teasing her, but she blushed just the same. She knew better than to ask for what they couldn't afford. "I was just pretending, Papa," she said. "It's lucky I don't need a straw hat, because I'm sure this one wouldn't fit me."

"Let's try it on and see," Papa said. He lifted the hat and held it above her while she pulled off her damp sunbonnet. When he set the straw hat on her head, it was as light as a breeze.

"You've earned a special treat today, Kirsten," Papa said. "I worried that we wouldn't have enough to sell for all the things we needed from Mr. Berkhoff. But when he saw that beeswax and tasted your honey, I knew we'd have enough and a little more besides. So you and Peter may each choose something for yourself."

"Peter, too?" Kirsten whispered. She was almost too happy to speak.

"He wants a knife," Papa said. "And you, Kirsten, would you like this straw hat?"

She nodded. Papa settled the hat on her head. Kirsten gazed in the looking glass and smiled at the blond girl in the straw hat who was smiling back. She saw Papa's face over her shoulder. Then, over her other shoulder, Kirsten watched Mama hand the baby to Aunt Inger and come to join them.

"What this hat needs is a nice ribbon and a little decoration," Mama said. She tied a length of black ribbon and a bunch of bright red cherries around it. Now there were three smiling faces in the looking glass.

Suddenly a ratatat of drums started up in the park. Fiddles joined the drums in a lively marching tune.

Peter ran outside. In a minute he was back in the open door of the store, with Caro on his rope right beside him. "It's the parade!" Peter shouted. "The parade is beginning right now! Come on, come on!"

Papa patted Kirsten on the shoulder. "Go on, wear your hat to the parade! A girl needs a straw hat on a day like this. I'll tell Mr. Berkhoff to add it to our account."

"Thank you, Papa!" Kirsten said. "Oh, thank you!"

"Take care that Peter doesn't get in the way of the horses," Mama told her. "Your Papa and I will be along in a moment."

Holding her hat on with one hand, Kirsten took Caro's rope from Peter. Caro's tail beat happily against her skirt as she and Peter hurried to join the crowd.

LOOKING BACK 1854

A PEEK INTO THE PAST

Frontier families worked hard to tame the wilderness.

Pioneers like Kirsten were surrounded by the wilderness. Outside their tiny cabins, the outdoors seemed to go on forever. Miles of forests were filled with trees. Millions of berries grew in thick prickly brambles. The prairie rolled on and on like an ocean of waving grass. Huge flocks of birds nested there and darkened the sky when they flew overhead. Their wings sounded like thunder.

A family like the Larsons got many things they needed from the land around them. From the forests, they took lumber for building their cabins and barns. There was plenty of wood to burn for cooking and heating, too. Pioneers hunted animals and found wild plants to eat. They fished in streams filled with fresh, clean water. The outdoors was generous to pioneers, who took all they could from it.

Farmers plowed strips of bare earth to stop prairie fires from spreading.

But pioneers wanted to do more than take what nature provided. They wanted to control the wilderness because they knew that living on its edge was dangerous. Summer lightning and winter snowstorms killed people who couldn't find shelter. Wild animals attacked. And pioneers knew they could starve if they relied only on wild plants and animals for food.

So families like the Larsons didn't just hunt and fish and gather wild fruits and berries. They also cleared the forests and prairies so they could plant and harvest their own crops. To do that, they lived and worked outdoors all day long for most of the year.

Being outdoors wasn't always fun. Winter was bitterly cold. Spring rains

Pioneers cleared the wilderness to plant crops. They hunted for food, too.

Hay spoiled quickly in the rain, so farmers hurried to get it indoors.

turned the ground to a sea of mud. And summer was hot and buggy. But pioneers had no choice. If they wanted to settle the wilderness, they had to work to control the land.

Children like Kirsten helped their families survive in the wilderness. They hunted for mushrooms, gathered berries, and fished. Sometimes they set traps and nets to catch small animals and birds, or hunted for the eggs of ducks or prairie chickens. Many of these jobs are things we do for fun today. Pioneer children enjoyed them, too. But they knew that they were doing important work.

Sometimes children stopped to play while doing their chores.

Their families counted on them to bring home food.

In the summer, when cabins were stuffy and hot, women often cooked meals and made preserves over outside campfires. Since pioneers didn't have fans or air conditioners, families often ate outside, too. It wasn't unusual for them to move tables and chairs outdoors to catch a passing breeze. They had nowhere else to go that was comfortable when the weather was hot. It was so warm inside tiny cabins without many windows that families sometimes stayed outside late into the evening, battling flies and mosquitoes as they waited for the air to cool. But they usually slept inside, for fear of wild animals.

In summer, pioneers cooked meals outside to keep cabins from getting too hot.

Frontier clothes didn't help people stay cool in the hot summer sun, either. Men and boys wore heavy boots and long pants to work outdoors. It wasn't proper for them to go without shirts in the 1850s. Women and girls wore dresses with full long skirts. Underneath, they were expected to wear at least

A girl's dress from the 1850s

one petticoat and a pair of pantalettes. They tried to keep their arms covered and wore sunbonnets to protect their faces from the sun, since a suntan was not considered ladylike. Children went barefoot, not for comfort but to save their shoes from wearing out.

Busy pioneers couldn't have imagined taking

Pioneer work clothes

A frontier town in Minnesota, 1855

long vacations like we do. They simply had too much work. And going camping in the woods like American families do today would hardly be a vacation for pioneers. To them, the woods were a reminder of all the land they still had left to clear. A trip to town would be a bigger treat. In fact, the only summer vacation a family like the Larsons would take was a one-day visit to the nearest town for a special celebration on the Fourth of July. In town they could visit with neighbors who lived too far away to see often. They could stop at the store and buy things they couldn't make for themselves. But most of all, in town pioneers could see the beginnings of a community. They could see that they were making progress in settling the wilderness.

This 33-star flag belonged to a pioneer family in 1859.

ORDER OF
EXERCISES
FOURTH OF JULY, 1857,
RIVER FALLS, WIS.